This book belongs to:

. . . .

 I read this book
once!

 I read this book
twice!

☆ I read this book
three times!

Retold by Gaby Goldsack

Illustrated by Ruth Galloway

Language consultants: Betty Root and Monica Hughes

This is a Parragon Publishing book
This edition published in 2007

Parragon Publishing
Queen Street House
4 Queen Street
Bath BA1 1HE, UK

ISBN 978-1-4054-9258-4
Printed in China

3

Hansel and Gretel

Notes for Parents

These **Gold Stars** reading books encourage and support children who are learning to read.

Starting to read

• Start by reading the book aloud to your child. Take time to talk about the pictures. They often give clues about the story. The easy-to-read speech bubbles provide an excellent "joining-in" activity.

• Over time, try to read the same book several times. Gradually, your child will want to read the book aloud with you. It helps to run your finger under the words as you say them.

• Occasionally, stop and encourage your child to continue reading aloud without you. Join in again when your child needs help. This is the next step toward helping your child become an independent reader.

• Finally, your child will be ready to read alone. Listen carefully and give plenty of praise. Remember to make reading an enjoyable experience.

Using your stickers

Remember to use the **Gold Stars** stickers at the front of the book as a reward for effort, as well as for achievement.

The fun color stickers in the center of the book and fold-out scene board at the back will help your child reenact parts of the story again and again.

Remember these four stages:

• Read the story to your child.
• Read the story **with** your child.
• Encourage your child to read **to you.**
• Listen to your child read **alone.**

8

I'm hungry.

Once upon a time there was a boy called Hansel and a girl called Gretel. They lived with their father and stepmother near a dark woods.

Their father was a poor woodcutter.

One day, there was no food to eat. They were all hungry.

9

That night Hansel and Gretel heard their father and stepmother talking.

There's no food to eat.

"There's no food to eat," said the woodcutter.

"Take Hansel and Gretel to the dark woods and leave them there," said the stepmother.

Leave Hansel and Gretel in the woods.

Gretel was scared.

Hansel had a plan.

He went outside and got some pebbles.

I have a plan.

12

The next day the woodcutter took Hansel and Gretel into the dark woods.

As they walked Hansel dropped the pebbles.

They walked deep into the dark woods.

"Stay here," said the woodcutter.

"I will come back."

The woodcutter did not come back.

Gretel was scared.

"Don't be scared,"
said Hansel.

"We can follow
the pebbles home."

I'm
scared!

Don't be
scared.

We can follow
the pebbles.

15

Hansel and Gretel followed the pebbles.

They were soon home.

The woodcutter was happy to see them.

The stepmother was not.

"Take them into the dark woods again," said the stepmother.

Hansel went to get some pebbles. The door was locked so he got some bread crumbs.

17

The woodcutter took Hansel and Gretel to the dark woods.

As they walked Hansel dropped the bread crumbs.

They walked deep into the dark woods.

"Stay here," said the woodcutter.

"I will come back."

The woodcutter did not come back.

Gretel was scared.

"Don't be scared," said Hansel.

"We can follow the bread crumbs."

But the birds ate the bread crumbs. Hansel and Gretel could not find their way home.

Hansel and Gretel were lost in the dark woods.

They walked until they saw a house.

The house was made of candy and cookies.

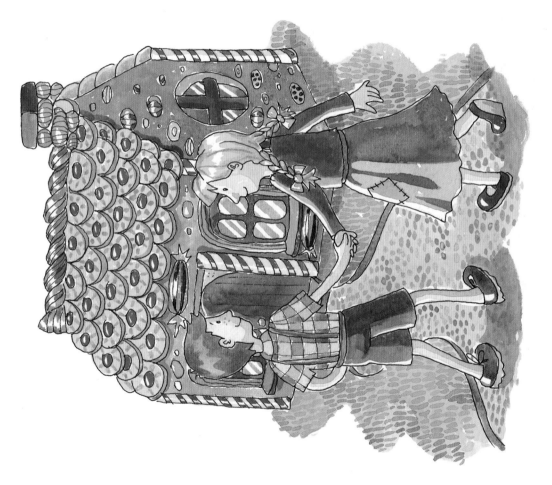

Hansel and Gretel were hungry.

They began to eat the house.

An old woman came out of the house.

"Come in," she said.

Yum! Yum!

Come in!

The old woman was a witch.

She locked Hansel in a cage.

She made Gretel feed Hansel.

She wanted Hansel to be fat enough to eat.

Every day the witch went to Hansel.

"Hold out your finger!" she said.

Hansel held out a thin chicken bone.

The witch could not see well.

"You're not fat enough!" said the witch.

Not fat enough!

One day the witch
could wait no longer.
She made Gretel heat
the water in the
big pot.

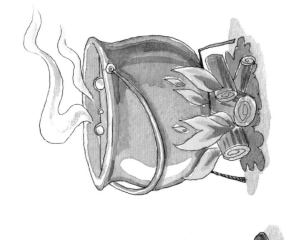

The witch looked
into the big pot to
check if the water
was hot. Gretel
pushed her in.

Gretel unlocked the cage.

Hansel and Gretel ran away.

They ran and ran all the way home.

Their father was happy to see them.

The stepmother had gone away.

They all lived happily ever after.

Read and Say

How many of these words can you say?

The pictures will help you. Look back

in your book and see if you can

find the words in the story.

woods

spoon

door

woodcutter

bread crumbs

stepmother

chicken bone

witch

pot

cage

29